THE YOUNG RIDERS:

CHASING VILLA'S GOLD

KEN HUDNALL AND SHARON HUDNALL

OMEGA PRESS
EL PASO, TEXAS

THE YOUNG RIDERS: CHASING VILLA'S GOLD

COPYRIGHT © 2019 KEN HUDNALL

OMEGA PRESS

http://www.kenhudnall.com

FIRST EDITION

Printed in the United States of America

OTHER WORKS BY THE SAME AUTHOR UNDER THE NAME KEN HUDNALL FROM OMEGA PRESS

MANHATTAN CONSPIRACY SERIES
Blood on the Apple
Capitol Crimes
Angel of Death
Confrontation

THE OCCULT CONNECTION
UFOs, Secret Societies and Ancient Gods
The Hidden Race
Flying Saucers
UFOs and the Supernatural
UFOs and Secret Societies
UFOs and Ancient Gods
Evidence of Alien Contact
Secrets of Dulce
Unidentified Flying Objects
Sensual Alien Encounters
Strange Creatures From Time and Space
Beyond Roswell
Alien Encounters
Mysteries of Space
Battle of Los Angeles
Is Someone On The Moon?
Intervention

DARKNESS
When Darkness Falls
Fear the Darkness

SPIRITS OF THE BORDER

(with Connie Wang)
The History and Mystery of El Paso Del Norte
The History and Mystery of Fort Bliss, Texas
(with Sharon Hudnall)
The History and Mystery of the Rio Grande
The History and Mystery of New Mexico
The History and Mystery of the Lone Star State
The History and Mystery of Arizona
The History and Mystery of Tombstone, AZ
The History and Mystery of Colorado
Echoes of the Past
El Paso: A City of Secrets
Tales From the Nightshift
The History and Mystery of Sin City
The History and Mystery of Concordia
The History and Mystery of ASARCO
Military Ghosts
School Spirits
Restless spirits
Railroad Ghosts
Nautical Ghosts
Haunted Hotels
Haunted Hotels in Arizona and Colorado
Ghosts of Albuquerque
The History and Mystery of Tucson
The History and Mystery of Santa Fe

SHADOW WARS
The Shadow Rulers
The Secret Elite

THE ESTATE SALE MURDERS
Dead Man's Diary
A Bloody Afternoon of Fun

BOOK OF SECRETS

Ancient Secrets
Secrets of the Dark Web

Northwood Conspiracy

No Safe Haven: Homeland Insecurity

Where No Car Has Gone Before

Seventy Years and No Losses: The History of the Sun

Bowl

How Not To Get Published

Lost Cities and Hidden Tunnels Along the Border

Vampires, Werewolves and Things That Go Bump in The

Night

Border Escapades of Billy the Kid

Criminal law for the Layman

Understanding Business Law

Language of the Law

Death of Innocence: The Life and Death of Vince Foster

The Veterans' Practice Primer

Unfinished Business

Mystery Men

PUBLISHED BY PAJA BOOKS
The Occult Connection: Unidentified Flying Objects

PUBLISHED BY PRUNE DANISH PRESS
Why Would They Say It?

DEDICATION

As with all of my endeavors, this would not be possible without the support and assistance of my lovely wife, Sharon Hudnall.

TABLE OF CONTENTS

CHAPTER ONE
A FORCED TRIP

It was a hot July afternoon in New York City in the year 1942, first year of America's involvement in the second world war. The needs of the military disrupted the lives of so many in America and the Phoenix family of Brooklyn, New York was about to have their lives completely changed.

"But I don't want to go," shouted 15-year-old Mark, his face red with both the stifling heat in the small apartment as well as with anger. "I don't want to get buried in the desert with a bunch of hicks! There are wild Indians and gunman there! We'll be killed."

"Mark!" patiently responded Dora Phoenix, his mother. "Your family, my parents and your cousins, are not hicks. They live on the edge of El Paso, Texas which is a fairly modern city as for wild Indians, the Indian wars ended sixty years ago. There are also no gunfighters left, that's just stuff from the movies."

Mark flung himself into the closest chair and folded his arms across his chest.

"OK, maybe we need to move from this apartment, but why do we have to move across the country," he demanded for the fifth time that afternoon. "This is our home, this is dad's home. He would not want us to move away. He told me that I was to look after the family until he got back and he's coming back here."

Dora took a deep breath and resolved to be patient.

"Mark, your father told you to be a man in this family in his absence, but a man has to look at the situation and face the facts. Without your father's income form the plant, we just don't have enough money to stay here and keep this apartment. What he sends home by his allotment from the military is not even half of what he used to make, there is just not enough money."

Mark was so frustrated that he slammed his right hand down on the top of the kitchen table, making both his mother and his younger brother, 14-year-old Karl jump.

"It's just not fair," he shouted, grabbing his hair with both hands. "He has to go off to war and fight over something that has nothing to do with us and we have to go live with hicks in the desert."

Dora took a deep breath and a firm grip on her temper.

"Mark, for the last time, my parents are not hicks. Who told you that they are hicks?"

Mark took a deep breath of his own and let it out, mumbling something under his breath.

Dora leaned closer to her son.

"What was that Mark? Who told you that folks in Texas are hicks?"

Mark realized that he had made a strategic error. He didn't want to answer but knew he had no choice.

"Well, it was Tommy Irwin from my school. His brother spent some time in Texas and knows that people there are real hicks. I don't want to spend my time with hicks and others of that type. Dad wouldn't want us to associate with that type of person."

Dora sat back in her chair and shook her head.

"Mark, how many times have I told you not to associate with Tommy Irwin and that gang he runs with?"

"They are not a gang, mother," objected Mark. "They are friends of mine, they have a club, that's all."

Dora's steely gaze skewered her oldest son.

"Don't tell me that they are not a gang, young man. Each one of them has been in trouble with the law since they were old enough to walk and you are not going to join them," she snapped. "I know from Mrs. Johnson down the hall that the older Irwin boy was in Texas alright, but he was in prison in Texas for robbery. He has no idea what real folks in Texas are like, just those in prison. No son of mine is going to associate with a jail bird."

She paused and forced herself to calm down. She knew that Mark could be stubborn if he was forced to do something against his will.

"Now Mark, you need to help me with this move, not fight me. That's what a man would do. Be glad that my parents have room for us and are willing to take in three more people until your father gets back from the war," she said in a voice that he brooked no further discussion.

With a grunt, he jumped from the table, ran into his room and slammed the door. He literally dove into his bed, face first, pounding the mattress with his fists in his frustration. He would not go to Texas, he just would not go, and no one could make him.

All of his dreams were going up in smoke because of this stupid war. He was going to get to pitch this coming school year on the school baseball team, the coach had promised him. Then there was that Sally McCormick that had let him kiss her behind the gym. So, what if she had been seen with every boy at the school, she liked him, she said so. All of these things he had dreamed of would be gone the minute he left. They had to stay in New York. He was still raging internally when he fell asleep.

CHAPTER TWO
A NEW RELATIVE

The next day was Saturday, so there was no school. Mark stumbled to the kitchen table, drawn by the smell of breakfast. His mother and brother were already eating, she had let him sleep longer than she normally did on the weekend.

He was still angry, but hunger overrode his plan to make everyone know that he was made at the world. Sullenly, he pushed food onto this plate and slowly ate it, after all his mother was a good cook. His mother looked at him and just shook her head. Karl ignored him and continued to pack away the food. Finally, his mother cleared her throat.

"Mark, we are going to Grand Central Station after lunch. My brother is coming in on the train. He is going to help us make the move to Texas."

Mark dropped his fork with a clang as it hit the side of the plate.

"But I don't want to go!" he exploded. "I will tell you right now that I am not leaving New York City."

Dora finally lost her temper at her oldest son.

"Mark Phoenix you will stop this attitude this instant," she yelled, her patience at an end. "I don't want to go any more than you do, but I have no choice. I can't make enough money to keep a roof over our heads with your father gone into the army. So, stop acting like a spoiled child and act like a young man. Help us make the best of the situation."

Tears streaming down her cheeks Dora Phoenix got up from the table went into her own bedroom and slammed the door. All of her worries about her husband at war and the money situation just overwhelmed her and she began to sob loudly. What was she to do?

Karl looked at his mother storm out of the kitchen and just shook his head as he got up from the table. He started for the door but paused to look at his brother.

"Mark, you may be the oldest, but you are also the dumbest. She cried all night about having to leave the city. You are just making it worse. It's not like she has a choice."

"Shut up, idiot," flared Mark, glaring at his younger brother. "Or I will pound you."

Karl smiled a sad smile at his brother, slowly shaking his head once again.

"And I suppose if you pound me that will make it all better? God you are such an idiot," Karl shot back.

With that he left the kitchen to return to his room. Now alone in the kitchen, Mark picked at his food before finally giving up and going back to his own room. Grabbing his jacket, he left the apartment, descending the stairs from their third-floor apartment to the street. Hands shoved in his pockets, head down, he walked slowly down the sidewalk, headed for the park. He loved the sounds of the traffic, some nights when he could not sleep, these were the sounds that lulled him to sleep. There had to be a way that his family could stay in New York City.

He brightened somewhat when he saw his friend Tommy Irwin and some of the other members of the club sitting on the edge of fountain in the park. When Tommy hailed him, he walked over to them.

"What's up, Mark?" asked Tommy, getting to his feet as Mark approached.

"Nothing, much, just getting some air," Mark responded, glumly.

"Your mon still going to take you to the ass end of nowhere out west and live with the hicks?" asked one of the boys with a smirk.

"Yeah, I guess," responded Mark with a deep sigh.

"Well, just don't go?" suggested Tommy, resuming his seat on the edge of the fountain.

Mark snorted.

"And do what?" he demanded. "How would I live in this city if I stay behind?"

Tommy smiled at his friend.

"Do what we do," he offered. "Steal."

"Steal?" questioned Mark, his mother's words coming back to him about these boys all being in trouble with the law. "Steal what, from whom?"

"Everything," offered another boy, Bruce Denier. "Unless you are a wimp."

A third boy raised his arm and pulled back the sleeve of his jacket to show a very ornate looking wrist watch.

"See this?" he demanded. "I stole if from old man Carter's jewelry store. It's easy to steal man. It's something called a Rolex. Everybody wants one and I bet I can get a bundle of cash for it when I am tired of showing it off."

"Yeah, Mark," interjected Tommy. "You can get a squat in one of the old tenements on the south end and steal what you need until you are old enough to get a job. Hell, my old man will hire you to run numbers for him in a year or two."

Mark looked at him curiously.

"What do you mean run numbers?"

He turned red when the others laughed at him, but Tommy patiently responded.

"My old man is a bookie. You collect bets and then if the people lose you go back and collect their losses. If they win, you go take them their winnings. The pay is good and the winners usually tip."

"That's not illegal?" asked Mark.

"Illegal, smeegle," retorted one of the other boys. "Who cares what the cops think."

"Yeah, what about it Mark?" asked Tommy Irwin. "You can stay behind, and I'll get my old man to give you odd jobs until you are old enough to be a runner."

Mark was tempted but then faced reality.

"Oh, who am I kidding," he said. "My mother will never let me stay behind."

"Hell, Mark," snorted Bruce Denier. "Run away from home and hide until your family leaves. We can help you hide."

Mark was very tempted to take him up on the offer, but he remembered his father making him promise to be the man of the family and look out for his mother and his brother. Running away was certainly not keeping his promise. He took a deep breath and slowly shook his head.

"Guys, I have to think about it," he responded. "That's a big decision."

"What's a matter, you chicken?" demanded Denier getting to his feet belligerently and advancing toward Mark. "You took much of a baby to leave momma's apron strings."

Denier was bigger and older than Mark, but though slim, Mark was muscular. Not wanting a fight, Mark started to turn to go when Denier grabbed him by the shoulder. Remembering lessons from his father during happier times, Mark grabbed Denier's wrist, turned and twisted. The other boy literally sailed through the air to go head first into the swirling waters of the fountain. The other boys watched in amazement.

"Don't ever grab me again, Denier," warned Mark, pointing his finger at the dripping boy who was now standing knee deep in the fountain, water dripping from his soggy clothes, his face red with anger.

He looked at Tommy Irwin who's face reflected his surprise at Mark's actions. "I'll let you know about your offer."

With that Mark turned and retraced his steps toward home, of course with a few side detours. He finally went home since he had to go to Grand Central Station with his Mother and brother to meet his uncle. At the same time, he replayed Tommy's words over in his mind. He could run away from home and live in the city by stealing. It had a romantic aura to it. Could he do it?

When he walked into the apartment, his mother met him at the door.

"So where have you been, young man?" she demanded. "We have to go in just a few minutes it we are going to meet my brother at the train station."

Mark shrugged, "Out," was all he said.

Dora threw her hands into the air in frustration.

"What am I going to do with you?" she demanded. "You know you aren't supposed to leave the apartment without letting me know here you are going. What if something happened to you?"

Mark only shrugged again, "Mom, I was just out, walking around. I am not a baby though that's how you treat me."

Dora's face fell as she remembered he was getting big, but with her husband gone, she did have the tendency to be over protective. She calmed herself as she got her keys and her purse.

"Okay, boys," she said. "Let's go meet my brother Peter. His train is due into Grand Central at noon. Try to be on your best behavior."

The three of them had to ride the subway into Manhattan in order to get to the train station, which meant the trip was long and tiring. Like most subways, it was always crowded, except in the early hours of the morning, and somewhat dirty. People pushed and shoved for the few seats, while most had to stand in the aisle and hold on to the overhead bars. On this Saturday afternoon, the crowds were tremendous, but at least there were no unexpected stops or power outages. Finally, after changing subways twice and then walking form the closest stop, they arrived at Grand Central Station, the hub of the trains in New York City.

Dora Phoenix and her sons checked the arrival board in the center of Grand Central and made their way to the correct track. They arrived just as a train whistle could be heard echoing down the track. They had arrived not a moment too soon.

The three stood back watching the people get off the train. Since this was a major line, as might be expected there was a veritable flood of people, but finally, Dora Phoenix raised up on her tip toes and waved frantically at a tall dark-haired man wearing a nice suit and a dark fedora. He was with an attractive woman, two girls and several suitcases sitting on the walkway beside the train. Mark, of course, had expected a man in cowboy boots with a big Stetson hat, but this looked nothing like he expected a man from Texas to look.

Leaving her two sons to follow, Dora fought her way through the crowd and threw herself in the arms of the big man. Standing slightly behind him was a blonde-haired woman and two tired looking young women. Mark absently noted that both younger women were attractive, though one was darker than the other and a real knockout. His attention was on the man hugging his mother.

Finally, Dora Phoenix pulled back and dabbed at her eyes with a handkerchief. The big man kept his arm around Dora and pulled the blonde hair woman into his other arm.

"Sis, good to see you!" he boomed as the two women hugged each other. "It's been a long time."

"I didn't expect the whole family to come to help us move," said Dora, wiping her eyes once again. "But I am sure glad to see you all."

Finally, Dora turned to her two sons.

"Boys, this is your Uncle Peter, his wife Margaret, their daughter Betty and Lucile, their ward."

Both boys dutifully shook Uncle Peter's hand and then had to submit to hugs from Aunt Margaret. The two girls, cousins Betty and Lucile, simply smiled at them from beyond the big Texan and the boys nodded in return.

Dora took a deep breath and grabbed the big man's arm.

"Let's get your luggage and then get on the subway," she said with a smile on her face. "I'm sorry but it is a long walk to the subway and then a thirty-minute ride."

Peter Puckett glanced at his wife and then turned to Mark and Karl.

"Why don't each one of you grab a suitcase and we will get a taxi. Save us all some shoe leather."

"Oh, Peter," objected Dora. "That's such an expense. We can take the subway."

"Nonsense, Dora," returned Margaret, taking her arm and pulling her toward the exit. "Let the men get the luggage and we will go meet the car service we called."

Dora looked like she was going to continue to object, but then shrugged and allowed Margaret to herd her along. The two boys just stood and watched them walked toward the exit followed by the two girls. They did not move until their Uncle spoke to them.

"OK, boys," he said. "Each of you grab two suitcases and I will get the rest of the bags."

Once they were all loaded down, Uncle Peter led the way toward the exit into which had vanished Dora and the rest of his family. "Leave it to women to pack three times what they need to bring on a trip."

As they exited the Station, they saw the boy's mother, Margaret and the two girls gathered around a large green van that had the word Puckett on a sign in the window. The driver was sanding waiting by the rear of the vehicle. Mark was surprised, he had never had someone use a car service, though he knew they existed in New York. Peter Puckett led the boys over and deposited all of the luggage on the ground by the driver.

"Here you go," he said with a sigh of relief. "I know it's a lot, but that's how my girls travel."

"Not a problem, sir," responded the driver, grabbing the first one and inserting it into the rear of the vehicle. "My name is Denny Martin from Martin's Car Service. We'll have you loaded and out of here in a just a minute."

He glanced over toward the ladies who were chattering up a storm.

"Why don't you all go ahead and get in, she'll hold all of you."

Leading the way, Margaret Puckett entered the van and grabbed a seat in the center bench. She motioned for the two girls to get in the third seat.

"Now leave room for the boys" she told her girls. "Dora, you sit here with me."

Obediently, Dora Phoenix slide into the center seat, leaning back with a sigh.

"I hate this expense, but I did dread the subway ride at this time of day," she said to no one in particular.

"Nonsense, Dora," responded Margaret patting her hands, which were folded in her lap. "We are here to help you. So shut up, sit back and be helped."

"That's my no nonsense, wife, Dora," laughed Peter. "She doesn't mince words."

Shortly the luggage was loaded, everyone in the van and the driver back behind the wheel. With a toot of his horn, the vehicle pulled away from the curb and merged with the traffic. Mark was still somewhat in awe that his Uncle, who he knew was from Texas did not dress or act like a hick. Maybe Tommy was wrong. Puzzled, Mark leaned his head against the window, very much aware of the press of his cousin, Lucile's, leg pressed against his own in the rear third seat. For the first time, he thought that maybe Texas might not be so bad.

CHAPTER THREE
THE TRIP TO TEXAS

Mark looked around his room, now empty of all of his stuff, just the furniture was left, which came with the apartment, left. The last few days had been a whirlwind, his uncle and aunt seemed to have everything in mind as they helped the overwhelmed Dora pack up all of the possessions gained in the last ten years and get it in the hands of the moving company. It took all week with all of them working hard, but finally, the apartment was empty of all of the things that made it home to Mark. Now the only things left to move were the people.

He half turned when someone came up behind him. He found that Lucile, his aunt and uncle's ward, had joined him. He was still surprised that she wasn't his blood cousin like Betty, and it had to be explained to him what a ward actually was. She had been placed in the care of the Puckett family when she was just a baby.

"Are you going to miss New York?" she asked him in her soft voice.

Mark glanced at her before answering. He found her soft brown skin exciting for some reason. He was surprised to find out that she was actually born in Mexico, but even so, he found that he just liked to look at her, which made no sense to him, but in spite of that he did.

"Well, yeah," he responded in a sad voice. "This is apartment is all the home that I have ever known and now I have to start over in a new town in a new state with people I barely know. No offense, but I really don't know any of you people, your father may be my uncle, but I have never met any of you prior to this. I am New York City, born and bred."

Lucile took a deep breath, smiled at him and gently rubbed his arm.

"No offense taken, Mark. Perhaps you can learn to like us and El Paso as much as you do New York City."

Not knowing what to say, he simply shrugged and turned his back on what had been his room and walked out, his head down. Lucile walked close by his side, sensing his pain.

Everyone but Betty was gathered in the living room. Dora was aflutter, making sure that she and the two boys had all of their luggage. There would be no coming back from this trip, so if they forgot something it was gone.

"Now, boys, have you packed everything?" she asked for the tenth time, as she pulled on her jacket.

"Yes, mom," responded Mark, defeat very clear in his voice. He had made one last effort the night before to remain behind, but Dora had been adamant that they would all go together. She had been horrified when he told you about Tommy Irwin's offer to get him a job as a numbers runner. Karl just nodded without responding.

At that moment Betty came in the door.

"The car is here," she announced breathlessly. "He's waiting to load the luggage.

Dora took a deep breath and smiled at her two sons.

"Time to start a new life," she chirped happily, picking up her suitcase and starting for the door, before Peter grabbed her bag from her hand.

"I'll take that," he said looking over his shoulder at the young people. "You all come along, no one gets left behind."

With a deep sigh of sadness, Mark picked up his own suitcase and started out the door, leaving the only life he had ever known.

As he reached the lobby of the building, he heard a sound and looked over his shoulder to see Tommy peering around the corner of the hallway leading to the back door.

"Psst – hey, Mark," he whispered loudly. "Come on, let's make a break for it."

Mark hesitated, looking through the glass front doors at his family loading their luggage into the car. He was sorely tempted, but finally he shook his head.

"Thanks, Tommy," he responded gratefully. "But my dad told me to take care of my mon and brother till he got back. This is something I gotta do for my dad."

Tommy looked at him long and hard before nodding.

"Be seeing you around," he said, disappearing into the hallway toward the back door.

Straightening his shoulders, Mark marched out the front to hand his luggage to the driver. With a long look down the street toward the park, his sighed and got into the car, again seated by Lucile in the last row of seats.

His life was over as he knew it, he told himself. As they pulled away from the curb, Mark refused to look back, afraid he would lose control and regret not making a break for it.

Grand Central Station was full of hustle and bustle as usual with people running for their trains and hordes of people coming from newly arrived trains. It was all that Peter, Margaret and Dora could do to get their little group across the grand concourse, down the tunnel to where their train was due to leave.

Though they left early, due to traffic and other delays, their train was getting ready to pull out of the station when they came from the tunnel to arrive track side. Mark had to marvel at his uncle using his size to make them a path through the crowded walkway. He had been pushed, shoved and buffeted to the point he regretted even more coming until Uncle Peter stopped by a conductor, handed him the tickets and ushered everyone on board.

The conductor followed them and shuffled through the sheaf of tickets in his hand.

"Oh, Mr. Puckett, I heard you were on this trip," he said, punching the tickets and handing them back to Mark's Uncle. "If you need anything let me know."

"Thanks, Henry," responded Peter Puckett, leading the way down the corridor. "Let's go folks, times a wasting."

In spite of himself, Mark was overwhelmed being on the train and even more surprised that the conductor knew his uncle's name. It was his first train ride, and he was going to cross the country. Not wanted to get separated from his family, Mark struggled to keep up as they pushed their way down a surprisingly crowded corridor almost to the end of the car. Finally, Uncle Peter opened the door to a room on the left.

"Betty, you and Lucile are in this room. Get settled since we will be on this train for two days until we switch in New Orleans to the Sunset Limited. Meet us in the dining car."

As the two girls entered, Uncle Peter led the way to the net door which he threw opened.

"Dora, Margaret, the three of us will have to share this room, there were not enough Pullman suites. But rest assured we have better accommodations on the Sunset Limited."

Finally, he got to the last doorway on the hallway and threw it open.

"Mark, Karl, this is your room," he said. "Get settled and then meet us in the dining car which is straight up this hallway into the next car."

Once the two boys were safely in the room, Peter turned and walked back to the room where he had left his wife and Dora Phoenix. The trip was about to begin.

Sitting his suitcase down by the door, Mark idly explored the room. There was a bench seat and then two chairs one on either side of the window that looked out onto the tracks and a small table between the two. A small door gave way to an attacked bathroom with a small shower.

With a sigh, he dropped into one of the chairs and idly watched the people pushing and shoving outside the car. In the back of his mind, he was still contemplating slipping off of the car and getting lost in the crowds in Grand Central Station. His mother and brother could go to Texas and he would stay here and run numbers for Tommy's dad. Everyone would be happy, but then what would he own father say. He had told him that he was the man of the family while he was gone to war and running out was not being a man. With another deep sigh, he realized that he was trapped.

Leaning back in the chair, he noticed that Karl was staring at him with those big brown eyes.

"Maybe it won't be so bad," Karl said. "But bad or not, you really have no choice but to go."

"I know," responded Mark, rubbing his face with both hands. "I had a chance to stay here and work for Tommy's dad running numbers. I could support myself and everything."

Karl looked at him steadily. "So, you would abandon us?"

Mark squirmed in his seat.

"No – well, uh - I just don't want to go to Texas, can't you understand?" He paused looking for a way to get his point across. "The city is my home, I love it."

Karl leaned back in his chair, his eyes following the people walking up and down the walkway outside the train window.

"Oh, I do understand," he responded softly. "Don't you think that I am going to miss the city? I think you are looking too much at what you want and not what it best for the family. As mom said, it is not like we really had a choice."

Before Mark could answer, the car jerked, and the train began to leave the station. The longest trip of their lives was underway.

Getting to his feet, Mark glanced down at his brother.

"Well, it doesn't matter now, so let's go to the dining car, I'm hungry."

The others were already sitting around a large table in the dining car when Karl and Mark joined them. There was a white coasted waiter standing nearby ready to take their orders. The two boys dropped into chairs beside their mother.

"Hope you boys are hungry," said Uncle Peter, "the food on this train is great."

Once everyone had placed their order, Dora bit her lip and turned to the two boys.

"I know that you don't want to leave, but we really have no choice. At least give Texas a chance," she began.

"Yeah," chimed in Lucile. "You'll love it. There are horses at the ranch for you to ride and a whole new world to explore."

"Ride a horse?" questioned Mark. "I have never even been near a horse."

"You'll love it," responded Betty, 'Lucile and I can teach you to tide."

At that moment, the waiter brought the drinks that they had each ordered and carefully sat them on the table. Dora toyed with hers for a moment before looking at her brother.

"Pete, I don't know how I can ever repay you for what this trip is costing you. It must be frightfully expensive."

Margaret laughed as she reached over to pat Dora's hand where it lay on the table.

"Nonsense, Dora," she responded. "First off you are family and secondly, didn't you know that Pete is employed by the railroad. The trip itself if free, courtesy of the Southern Pacific. He has family passes, so that is not an issue."

"So that's why the conductor knew you," interrupted Mark.

Peter smiled and nodded his head.

"Yep, I am a senior vice president based in San Antonio. When I knew that you were going to be making this trip, I took my vacation to come get you. So, don't even think about cot, we are all family. Family helps family."

"Well I just want to say that I – we – are eternally grateful," offered Dora. "I don't know how we would have done it without your help."

Some help thought Mark sourly, as he glanced out the window and saw that they were almost at the outskirts of New York City. He was leaving home and felt he would never see it again.

CHAPTER FOUR
A NEW HOME AND A NEW FRIEND

The trip was almost three days to New Orleans with numerous stops along the way and then they switched trains to the Sunset Limited for the rest of the trip. It was another two days before the train pulled into El Paso's Union Station. As Mark stepped down from the car it almost felt strange not to have the floor move beneath him. He had become used to the gently swaying of the Pullman car as it whipped along the track.

Hoisting his suitcase, he followed Uncle Pete and the rest of the crowd across the concourse out to the parking lot. There they all piled into a station wagon, which he saw had what appeared to be wooden sides. Betty noticed him looking curiously at the car and laughed.

"It's called a woody because of those wooden panels on the side of the car," she explained.

Uncle Pete heard her explanation and nodded.

"That's right, boys," he said, "I was going to get a new car, but production of civilian vehicles has been suspended for the duration so that the car factories can produce military vehicles. Besides old woody still has a lot of miles left in him. So, sit back, we have about an hour drive."

Without responding, Mark slid into the backseat. It was worse than he had imagined, they would not even be living in town but way out in the sticks. Perhaps Tommy Irwin was right.

The adults sat in the front seat while the four teenagers were crammed into the back. The luggage took up the rear of the station wagon. With the windows down for what air cold enter the car, they went roaring along first a narrow road then on several dirt roads.

Finally, after what seemed like an age, they turned into a narrow dirt road and went beneath an archway that said Puckett Ranch. In the distance, Mark could see a two-story ranch house that seemed to stretch in both directions. It was huge. Mark glanced around but all he saw was desert in every direction. His worst fears were realized, he was in the sticks and anyone living in the sticks was a hick.

Pete Puckett drove around the right side of the house to a large garage in the back and stopped in front of it. Standing on the large back porch were an older couple and two Mexicans wearing big hats. As they began to pile out of the car, the four approached.

Dora rounded the car and was engulfed in the arms of the older man and woman. Mark realized that they were probably his grandparents. The woman looked like an older version of his mother. When Mark and his brother got out of the car they were immediately grabbed by the older woman and had to endure tight hugs and wet kisses on their cheeks. The older man just offered a weather roughened hand for them to shake.

"Howdy, boys," said the old man in a deep gravelly voice. "I'm your grandfather, Amos Puckett. You can call me grandpa, granddaddy or whatever you want to call me."

He paused and studied both boys intently with his bright blue eyes for a moment.

"You," he said pointing at Mark, "must be Mark and that makes you Karl."

Mark said nothing, but Karl laughed and nodded his head.

Jean, Puckett, her arm around Dora again looked over at her husband.

"Well, take them into the house, old man" she said. "It's hot out here."

Without a word, Amos turned and led the way, his cowboy boots raising little puffs of dust as he walked. The two Mexican helpers grabbed the luggage and took it into the house. As they walked Pete leaned down close to Mark's ear and whispered, "Don't worry, his bark is worse than his bite."

"And I got good damn hearing, too," snapped the old man over his shoulder as he led the way.

Uncle Pete looked at Mark, grained and winked.

Once he had been shown the way to his room and unpacked his luggage, Mark was at a loss for what to do. He was surprised to have been give his own room on the second floor. The house was huge, it seemingly went on forever. Karl had a room next door and was loud in voicing his satisfaction. Mark was happy with his room as far as that went, but when he looked out the window, he saw a lot of nothing, not the teeming streets of the city that he had grown up with. He was bored already.

Getting to his feet, he left his room and descended the stairs to the kitchen. The adults were all gathered around the kitchen table chatting. Not finding the discussion interesting, Mark went through the kitchen and out into the yard. He decided he may as well explore.

Seeing a building set back form the house he decided to start there, of course before he got there, he knew that it had animals from the smell. He had smelled something similar at the zoo in the city. The double doors were standing open, so he stuck his head inside and saw an older man working on what he knew was a saddle. Sensing he was not alone, the workman looked up and spotted Mark.

"Hello, young fella," said the man, continuing to work on the saddle. "You must be one of the Phoenix boys, Mr. Amos's grandkids."

Mark stepped fully into the stable breezeway.

"Yes sir," responded Mark. "I'm Mark."

Putting his tools down and getting to his feet, the man reached out to shake Mark's hand.

"I'm Manny Alvarado, foreman at the ranch," he said.

Mark wrinkled his forehead.

"Pleased to meet you, sir. I'm sorry for my ignorance, but what's a foreman?" he asked.

"Well, that means that I am in charge of the workers," he responded. "And let's forget about the sir. I am Manny."

Mark nodded his understanding as he glanced around the breezeway. He could see several doors along both walls and heard what sounded like movement from behind the nearest one. He looked at Manny Alvarado curiously.

"What's that behind the door?" he asked curiously. "Sounds like something big moving around inside."

"Why, that one of the horses," the older man responded in a surprised voice. "there are a number of them on the ranch."

"Oh," responded Mark, looking around the stable. "I've never been up close to a horse. I've only seen pictures and the horses that pull the carriages in Central Park in New York."

Alvarado laughed and motioned for Mark to follow him.

"Well, follow me, young man and I will introduce you to the best friend that you can ever have," as he led the way deeper into the stable.

Mark followed obediently almost halfway down the breezeway and stopped in front of one of the doors. Reaching up, Alvarado turned a handle and the top half of the door opened. Inside, Mark could see a blonde looking horse, who raised his head and snorted.

"Mark Phoenix, I want you to meet Queenie," he said motioning for Mark to step closer. "She's my personal favorite and as gentle as they come. She's older but still full of pep and stamina."

Cautiously reaching forward, Mark drew his fingers along the side of her neck as she leaned out to nuzzle the side of his face. He laughed at the feel of the horse's hot breath on the side of his face.

As Mark became more comfortable with petting the horse, he looked over at Manny, who was standing behind him.

"Who does she belong to?" he asked curiously.

Manny Alvarado smiled at the boy.

"Well, frankly you, if you want her," he responded.

Mark couldn't believe his ears. He forgot all about being homesick in the excitement of having his own horse.

"Do I ever," he responded excitedly. "Of course, I want her."

He paused and his face fell.

"But I have no idea how to ride a horse," he said sadly.

Manny laughed and reach over to give Queenie a pat on her neck.

"Well don't let that stop you," he responded. "Mr. Amos wants me to teach both of you boys how to ride and care for a horse. So, I guess we can start with you."

So it was that Manny Alvarado spent the rest of the afternoon instructing Mark how the care for a horse, everything from the proper way to use a hoof pick to the way to properly groom, feed and putting a bridle and a saddle on the animal. After three hours, Mark was tired but elated when he finally was allowed to properly mount Queenie in the breezeway.

At first, he was terrified when Manny Alvarado led the horse out into the fenced are behind the stable and turned her loose. Mark held the reins in one hand as Manny had shown him and then gently tapped her sides with the heels of his shoes. Slowly and then a little faster, Queenie began to walk around the fenced arena. To Mark it was unbelievable that such a huge creature was obeying his commands.

Things were going great and then he noticed that the two girls and Karl had come to the fence and were watching him ride. Surprisingly, he found that he was inordinately proud of being able to ride and tapped his heels on her sides again, urging her to go a little faster. Then the unthinkable happened.

Manny was leaning in the doorway to the stables when one of the feral cats that lived in the stable came dashing out and underneath Queenie's hooves. Startled, the horse bucked, and Mark went sailing off the saddle to hit the ground on his back, knocking the wind out of his lungs.

The girls climbed the fence and Manny came running from the stable to help him get to his feet.

"Are you hurt, Mark?" demanded Lucile as she brushed the dust off of his back.

Still not able to talk, Mark couched and shook his head. As he straightened, he was surprised to feet Queenie's soft nose rub his cheek. He looked up to see that the horse had come back to him and was nuzzling his face. Though now scared of her, he forced himself to put his hand on her mane.

Manny grabbed her bridle, though she showed no signs of wanting to wander away.

"This is her way of saying she's sorry for throwing you," he said. "she didn't mean too, the cat scared her. Want to get back on?"

Mark hesitated, forcing himself to be calm. Finally, he nodded and took the reins. Walking to Queenie's side, he raised his foot and stuck it into the stirrup, jumping to swing his other leg over Queenie's back. This time, he was more cautious in urging her forward. But he rode steadily without any other problems for another half an hour or so before Manny waived him over to the stable.

"That's enough for today, Mark," said Manny holding Queenie's reins while Mark dismounted. "I'll groom Queenie and feed her tonight, besides, you are going to want to take a hot bath tonight or you will be sore in the morning from hitting the ground."

As Manny started forward with Queenie in tow, the horse turned and nuzzled Mark once again.

"Well, boy, she likes you," laughed Manny. "You have to always watch what you are doing, just as you depend on her, she depends on you to watch to make sure that nothing hurts or scares her."

As Mark watched Manny lead Queenie back to her stall, he realized that for the first time since he had been told about the move, he was actually happy. He really enjoyed having a horse and learning to ride.

He turned to see the three standing behind him.

"You did good, Mark," said Betty.

"We've all been thrown at least once," said Lucile. "Don't let it bother you."

"I want to ride," said Karl, looking wistfully at Queenie as Manny led her into her stall.

CHAPTER FIVE
AN OLD MAN'S TALE

Most city boys would consider leaving the glitz and glamour of New York City to come to what Mark had originally believed was the back side of nowhere to be a sort of punishment, but Mark Phoenix had discovered to his surprise that he loved to listen to his grandfather spin one of his yarns and ride across the prairie on the horse he had been given.

Mark did not understand the whole story, but he knew that it was a lack of money that brought his family to live with his grandparents and had fought against coming. They had lived in a nice apartment in Brooklyn, buy after his father had been drafted to join the military, there had not been enough money coming in to pay all of their bills. So, the three of them had been forced to move clear cross the country to live permanently with his grandparents. His mother had promised them that once his father returned from the war they would move back to New York.

They had now been on the ranch for about six weeks. Karl was not exactly happy, but Mark was discovering that he was actually enjoying the move, though he would not admit it. He had never known his grandparents and found that he always enjoyed listening to the old man, as they called his grandfather, talk about how things actually had been in the west back when he was young, especially the stories of hidden treasure just waiting to be found. The stories ranged from Indian attacks to outlaw shootouts, all of which Mark found fascinating, to him it was better than the movies. Karl found the stories boring beyond belief but was too polite to say it out loud.

Today, after lunch, Mark's grandfather, Amos Pickett, was talking about the famous Mexican Bandit, Pancho Villa. Along with Mark, there were his cousins all sitting around Amos' chair. His brother had wandered out into the yard rather than listen to what he called his grandfather's fairy tales.

"Yes sir, as a very young man Pancho Villa used to work at the old ASARCO Smelter down by the Rio Grande on the outskirts of El Paso." The old man paused to sip from his mug of coffee.

"He would come across the border every day and put in a good 8 to 10 hours hauling ore for the plant before going back home to Mexico. He was a good, dependable worker according to all reports. But that was long before he became a general during the Mexican Revolution.

There were a lot of stories about him, after he became famous in Mexico, attending dances in town and dining out in some of El Paso's finest restaurants. In fact, according to my father, who served with General Black Jack Pershing, Villa was best friends with General Pershing in spite of the fact that Pershing chased him across most of Mexico after Villa's troops attacked Columbus, New Mexico."

The old man paused and leaned back in his chair, his thoughts clearly about the past rather than the present.

After a long period of silence, Mark dared to prompt the old man.

"What about the treasure, grandfather?" he asked softly.

The old man started and grinned.

"Sorry, I sort of drifted off," he responded, taking another sip of his coffee. "That's what happens when you get old."

"You're not really old, grandpa," offered 15-year-old Betty, with a smile of her own. 'You're just experienced."

The old man laughed loudly, crossed his legs and favored his grandkids with a fond smile of his own.

"Well. I guess you could say that I am very experienced," he replied.

"How old are you, grandpa?" asked 14-year-old Lucile, Betty's foster sister, her parents' ward.

"Well, kids, I will be seventy years old the day before Christmas." He replied.

"Can we get back to the story?" urged Mark, annoyed at the silly questions from his cousins.

"Oh yes," replied the old man, rubbing his chin with his right hand. "Now, where was I?"

"You were going to tell us about the treasure left by Pancho Villa," replied Mark.

"Right. Well, Pancho Villa became a great General during the Mexican Revolution. He even had his own army that was loyal to him, not the government of Mexico. Many said that he used the revolution as an excuse to rob and kill to feather his own next and feather it he did.

From Sinaloa to the Chihuahua desert to Sonora, his troops stole anything that wasn't tied down and even a few things that were. A mountain of gold and silver were turned over to Villa by his loyal troops. However, when he was killed none of it could be found."

"What happened to it?" demanded Mark, leaning forward, ignoring the smirks of his cousins at his excitement. It suddenly dawned on him that if he could find the treasure, he could move back to New York City. That treasure would be the answer to all of his problems.

"Well, Villa was smart, he knew that the state of affairs that allowed him to rob and kill without having to answer for his crimes could not last forever, because the revolution could not last forever. So, he sent some loyal troops north of the border to hide a lot of it here in Texas."

"Where?" demanded Mark.

The old man smiled the smile that had charmed dozens of young ladies in his youth.

"Well. Mark, that's the thing, no one knows where it was hidden. As far as anyone knows it had never been found."

"There were no clues at all?" responded the boy.

The old man hesitated. "Well, according to my daddy, who was a Texas Ranger at the time, Villa sent a small unit consisting of six of his soldiers, north to hide the treasure on this side of the border, so if he ever had to run, he could dig it up and live like a king here.

This small unit was commanded by a very loyal Lieutenant, so Villa trusted him to not run off with the treasure. The troops left from Durango, Mexico and crossed the border near Zaragosa and rode in this direction. When they reached a particular canyon, the Lieutenant had the six soldiers dig a large hole and bury the treasure. When they were all involved in the digging, he shot all six, pushed their bodies into the hole and covered them up. On a nearby boulder, he scratched the word ORO, which is Spanish for gold. The Lieutenant also made a map of the location and took it back with him to Mexico, to present to Villa. The same night he arrived back at Villa's headquarters, the Lieutenant died, so only the map can show where the treasure was buried."

"Wow," breathed Mark. "Why did the Lieutenant shoot those men?"

"He shot them so that no one would know where he had buried the treasure. Apparently, Villa did not want anyone to know besides himself that's why the Lieutenant was killed."

"Man, if we could find that treasure it would solve all of our problems," breathed Mark, picturing digging up a mountain of gold coins.

"Yeah, well me and my daddy looked for it for years and never found it," responded the old man, getting to his feet. "You young folks go amuse yourselves, I'm gonna lie down."

Wanting to know more, but not wanting to take the chance of angering his grandfather, Mark allowed the two girls to herd him out of the large living room. The house had been built in the late 1800s and was a large two-story adobe ranch house, though with Mark and his family living there it was a tad cramped.

When they entered the kitchen, their grandmother Jean and Mark's mother were sitting at the kitchen table. They both looked up and smiled at the children.

"Enjoy your story?" asked Dora, with a twinkle in her green eyes.

"Oh yes, though Mark was hypnotized," laughed Betty, grabbing a glass and running it full of water from the kitchen sink. "He really believed it was true."

Stung, Mark snapped back at her.

"Well, if we could find that treasure, it would solve all of our problems," he responded.

"Well, don't get your hopes up, young man. Your grandfather means well, but sometimes his stories are made up out of whole cloth," said his grandmother, a cup of coffee held in one hand. "Just remember, they are just stories."

"My daddy's been telling stories as long as I can remember," laughed his mother, nursing her own cup of coffee between her cupped hands. "It would be nice if they were all true, but sometimes they are factual and sometimes they are just stories. Besides, he is getting up in years and his memory is not what it used to be."

"Well, I believe him," said Mark as he stormed out the back door, the laughter of his cousins ringing in his ears. He was determined to prove that he was right about his grandfather's stories.

CHAPTER SIX
THE HIDDEN ROOM

Angrily, Mark stomped across the yard toward the stables, his cowboy boots, a gift from his grandparents, making deep impressions in the dirt. He planned to saddle up and ride out across the desert, something that always made him feel better. However, at the last minute, he heard his brother laughing and talking with someone inside the stable. The last thing he wanted at this point was his brother to laugh at him as well.

So it was that he finally sought refuse in the old pit house that had been dug into the side of the hill behind the main ranch house long ago. Mark remembered his grandfather telling him that it had been the first structure built on the ranch and that J.D. Puckett, Mark's great-grandfather had always called it his special place and no one else ever used it.

Though the door had been locked with a big padlock, being a typical curious kid, it had taken Mark only a few short hours to find a way into the old building, but to his disappointment, instead of something valuable, it had only contained an old desk, a book case and a chair inside. He had hoped that something special or exciting had been hidden there. Still, it was his secret place that no one else ever entered

Now, in his anger, Mark entered the building, shouldering open the front door and slamming it as hard as he could in his anger. He smelled the musty smell that he long associated with hidden places. He froze when he heard something crash in the darkness, since he had no idea what it could be. With the door shut, the interior of the dugout was dark, as the two windows were tightly barred.

Feeling his way over to where he knew the desk sat, he felt around until he found the matches he had brought on an earlier trip and struck one. In that dim light he found the old lantern that sat by the door and lit it.

Raising the lantern high, he looked around the interior and found that the slamming of the door had caused a section of the wall to the right of the desk to come loose and fall to the floor. That was startling enough but what he saw behind where that section of wall had been sent a chill down his back, it was a small hidden room. Picturing the outside in his mind, Mark realized that the hidden room was completely buried in the hillside, and as far as he knew, no one living knew that it was there. When his grandfather had been giving him the tour of the ranch when he arrived, he was sure that he would have been shown this room if anyone knew that it was there.

But then he thought about it and realized that his grandfather had never even mentioned the old dugout. Mark had found it on his own while exploring the ranch buildings. In fact, the entrance had been covered with brush. Mark had found the doorway only because he was chasing one of the feral cats that had stolen his sandwich and the cat had come this way.

Bending over, Mark slowly entered the hidden room, placing his feet carefully on the dirt floor. The room was only about six feet across and five feet wide. The first thing he saw was an antique rifle hanging on a rack on the far wall, a pistol belt of dark leather hanging from a peg, in the holster, he could see the butt of a pistol. There was a small work table beneath it. On the top of the table was a book and some old papers.

But it was what was on top of those papers that caught his attention. On top of the papers he saw something gleaming in the lantern light. Leaning forward, he sat the lantern on the table and picked up one of the gleaming items. To his amazement, he saw that he was holding a gold coin.

In fact, there were six of the gold coins laid out side by side on the table.

Slowly, almost reverently, he turned his attention to the book and the papers, themselves. Gently he opened the cover of the book to see that someone had written J.D. Puckett in a flowing hand. Carefully turning a few pages, Mark discovered that it was a dairy, apparently that of his great-grandfather. The papers lying beside it turned out to be a wad of faded newspaper clippings.

Gently, Mark turned the pages of the dairy, the ink was somewhat faded, but still legible, though the handwriting was something of a scrawl. By the light of the sputtering lantern, Mark slowly read the words of his great-grandfather.

July 24, 1934: *"I probably should have told my son, but I finally found some of Villa's treasure. It wasn't the big one that he had the Lieutenant bring over, but it was big enough. I suspect that it was the proceeds of the Army paymaster robbery that I heard about.*

I know from a friend of mine at Fort Bliss that Villa did rob the paymaster as he was heading for the post. The amount of gold and silver coins taken in that robbery was close to $150,000.00 in gold and silver coins. Lord knows what those coins would be worth today. Naturally that much gold and silver weighed a considerable amount and Villa discovered that due to the weight he was not going to make it to the river before the pursuing cavalry caught him. So, according to the story, he buried the gold close to the river figuring on coming back to get it later. Well, he never did return to dig up the gold.

Me and old Ned tracked the clues and finally we found the stolen gold hidden by Villa on a bluff near the river crossing. We both took an oath to tell no one what we had found until we could be sure that the Army wouldn't try to take the gold back. Since it had been almost twenty years since the robbery, we are probably safe, but I don't want to take any chances. We hid the gold at Indian Springs and Ned stayed to guard it while I went to Fort Bliss.

July 26, 1934: Came back to our camp and that old fool tried to shoot me. I was faster, but he winged me. He had packed the gold onto several burros and apparently was going to hide it from me. So, I moved it to skeleton cave and buried it in the side tunnel, marked the spot with a shovel. I left the old fool lying in our old camp.

Soon as I heal up, I'll go back and get the gold. Didn't want to chance bring it to the house until I knew what the score was."

July 27, 1934: Borrowed $10,000.00 from that old skinflint Mort Harris at the bank, pay it back as soon as I recover the treasure.

July 30, 1934: Cashed in several of the coins from the cache. Paid back that old skinflint at the bank with interest. Put the rest of the coins and the receipt for the loan repayment for safekeeping at State National Bank in El Paso. Got one of them new-fangled safety deposit boxes and paid the fee for 10 years. Check with Bob for the key to that box.

Mark turned the page and discovered that this was the last entry. Slowly, he closed the journal and got to his feet. So, his great grandfather really had found some of Villa's treasure only to have his partner try to kill him. Now the question was were had he hidden it. Mark had never heard of Skeleton Cave, but perhaps his grandfather would know where it was.

Getting to his feet, Mark's eyes were drawn to the rifle hanging over the table. Gently, he picked it up and ran his hands over the gleaming barrel. It was covered with some type of grease, but it still shown in the lantern light. He worked the action and to his surprise an unspent shell was ejected to land on the table.

Easing the hammer down, he returned the rifle to its place on the wall and pulled the pistol from the holster. The pistol hand ivory handles with what looked like the Texas Ranger star inlaid in what appeared to be silver. Fingering open the gate, Mark discovered that the pistol was still loaded so he thumbed close the gate and gently returned the pistol to the holster.

Gathering the journal and the clippings, Mark left the room, carefully hiding the door to the hidden room. Cracking open the outer door, he made sure no one was in the yard before he walked carefully and quickly to the back door and as silently as possible entered and made his way to his room without seeing anyone.

Gently closing the door to his small room located on the second floor of the old house, Mark gently laid the journal on the table beneath the window and proceeded to read each and every entry. Apparently, J.D. Puckett lived an exciting life. To his surprise, he found that he liked his great-grandfather though he had never met him.

The journal covered the years 1924 to 1934 and in it the old man had recorded each and every adventure that he had experienced. As a Texas Ranger, he had been involved in some very exciting things from chasing criminals to exploring little known areas of the prairie. Mark was suddenly proud to be descended from this man. But what frustrated him was that nowhere in the journal did it give any clues about the location of Skeleton Cave.

Finally, he turned to the clippings, most of which were faded and hard to read, but the headline on one took his breath away. It said AMERICAN TELLS STORY OF FINDING VILLA LOOT WORTH FABULOUS FORTUNE. The article below the headline, as best as Mark could make out, was about a man named C.F. Degner who claimed that he had found a map showing where all of Villa's treasure caches were hidden.

Mark lowered the clipping he was reading with one thought in his mind. This was evidence that the treasure was real, now if he could just find it, their problems would be solved, and they could go back to New York and live in style.

CHAPTER SEVEN
A PROBLEM AND A TREASURE HUNT

The next morning Mark slept late, having studied a map of the area most of the night looking for Skeleton Cave. He finally came into the kitchen to find that the entire family was sitting around the breakfast table, though no one was eating. He noticed that his Aunt Flora and Uncle Pete, his mother's brother, were present and everyone looked depressed.

"Did I miss something?" asked Mark curiously grabbing a biscuit off of the plate in the center of the table.

"Nothing for you to worry about," responded his mother leaning over to ruffle his hair affectionately. "Why don't you go join your brother and cousins outside and go for a ride."

He started to say something but suddenly realized that the grownups wanted to talk. Grabbing another biscuit, he walked out into the yard to see his cousins and brother by the stable.

"Well, I see you finally woke up, squirt," quipped his brother. "they chase you out of the house as well?"

"Yeah," responded Mark, what's going on?"

Betty looked to make sure that no one was watching from the kitchen windows.

"Well, I heard my daddy talking to grandpa, it seems that great grandpa borrowed $10,000.00 from the bank and the note is being called due. Mr. Harris has given grandpa thirty days to pay or they are taking the ranch."

Mark was stunned.

"But that money was borrowed 8 years ago, why are they just now calling the note?" he protested. "Besides, great grandpa paid the note off and got a receipt."

He suddenly froze as all three turned to look at him curiously.

"How did you know that the money was borrowed 8 years ago? Not even grandpa knew that?"

"Uh, well, I guessed," he stammered.

Karl looked at him with that old look.

"Ok, Mark, out with it. What do you know?" he demanded. "How do you know that the note was paid off?"

Mark squired but finally was forced to confess.

"I found great grandpa's journal in a hidden room in the dugout. He mentioned that he borrowed the money and paid it off."

All three looked at him in amazement.

"A hidden room?" demanded Karl. "What dugout?"

"You read his journal?" demanded Betty.

"The loan is paid off?" asked Lucile. "When?"

"Prove it Mark," demanded Karl.

Left with no other choice, Mark returned to the house, followed by the other three. He walked past the family meeting and returned to his room. Picking up the journal, he returned to the kitchen and laid it in front of Amos Puckett.

"Grandpa, I was just told about the bank calling the note, but the note is paid off," said Mark before anyone else could say a word.

"What's this?" asked Amos, his work roughened fingers picking up the journal.

"It's your daddy's journal that I found hidden in the dugout," responded Mark.

Everyone at the table this looked at him in total amazement.

"Dugout?" asked Pete, "What dugout?"

Amos cleared his throat and glanced at his son.

"There's an old dugout behind the stables. It was the first building on the ranch. Daddy used it as an office, but it was boarded up when he died," he responded. He glanced at Mark.

"How did you find that?" he asked mildly.

Mark squirmed nervously.

"Well I was eating a sandwich one afternoon and one of those cats grabbed it and took off. I chased him through the hedge and into a hole in the hillside. At the back of the hole was a door with a padlock. I picked the lock and got inside," he responded.

Finally, his mother spoke.

"You went into that old hole in the ground!" she demanded, her voice angry. "You could have been injured or killed inside that old shed. You could have been bitten by a rattlesnake. You could-."

She stopped speaking when Amos raised one hand. He held the journal out to Mark.

"Where does it say that the note is paid off?" he asked quietly.

Mark took the journal and turned to the last entries. He pointed to the last one.

"Here it says that he paid the note and put the receipt into a safety deposit box at State National Bank in El Paso."

Amos quietly read the entry again and again. Peter Puckett looked confused.

"If it was paid off 8 years ago, why is James Harris trying to foreclose on the note now, especially if J.D. paid it off?"

Jean Puckett took a deep breath and shook her head.

"J.D. Puckett was a hard man. He was a Texas Ranger and a bounty hunter from time to time. One of the men he brought to justice was old Mort Harris's youngest son Homer. James was Mort's oldest son and followed his father to be president of the Cattleman's Bank. This could be an attempt to pay us back for what happened to Homer."

"What happened to Homer?" asked Karl.

"He robbed his own daddy's bank and headed for Mexico. Mort was going to replace the money out of his own pocket, but J.D. went after Homer and brought him back. He went to trial and was found guilty. The jury sent him to prison where he died. Mort never forgave J.D. for that."

Amos ran his hand gently over the cover of the old journal.

"I knew that my daddy kept journals, but I have only seen one of two. Where did you find this, Mark?"

"When everyone laughed at me for believing your treasure story, I was going to go riding, but then I decided to go into the old dugout. I have been in it many times and it's snug and warm. Today, I went in and slammed the door and a piece of the wall fell off and I saw a door. I lit the lantern that was out there and went into the room. There was an old worktable, a rifle and a pistol hanging on the wall and this journal and some clippings."

Amos pursed his lips and sighed.

"Daddy always said that was his special place and forbid anyone else to go inside. Frankly, I have only been in it once or twice. After he died, I could never find his rifle and pistol, I guess he left them in his special place."

The old man looked up at his grandson.

"Mark, that's your special place now. I think my father would have been proud to have you use his place as your own."

He looked over at Mark's mother.

"The structure is sound and there are no unwelcomed visitors, just dirt and spiders."

He looked back at Mark.

"The rifle and pistol, if they are the ones I am thinking of, were presented to him by his Ranger company. They are yours, boy. Bring them into the house and put them in my gun case."

"But dad," objected Mark's mother.

"To be used only under my supervision," finished Amos, anticipating his daughter's objection. "This is the west; a boy needs to learn the skills of a man."

Idly Amos flipped through some of the other entries in the old journal and then froze as he read the ones mentioning the treasure.

"Mark," he asked slowly. "Did you find anything else in the dugout?"

Mark hesitated and then slid his hand in his pocket, closing his fingers around the items he carried. Withdrawing his hand, he carefully laid the item he held on the table. When he withdrew his hand the gold coin seemed to glow with an inner fire. Everyone in the room was stunned to silence.

"Where did you get that?" demanded his mother, reaching out for the coin, but not quite touching it. "Is it real?"

"It was sitting on the old work table in the hidden room. Great-grandpa found one of Villa's treasures like it says in his journal," responded Mark, being careful not to mention how many coins had been there. His daddy had always said put something back for a rainy day.

"Uh," was all his mother could say.

Amos smiled at the folks around the table.

"Well, Daddy did always let on that he had a secret, but no one knew what it was. I guess this was it."

The old m at looked at his son.

"Pete, you and me, got to make a trip into the bank to see James Harris and end this foolishness about the note. But first, we got to go to the State National Bank and see if there really is a safety deposit box. I never knew daddy to have that much to do with banks, but maybe he did."

"Grandpa, who is Bob?" asked Mark.

The old man stopped and finally shook his head.

"I don't know any Bob, why do you ask?"

Mark opened the journal and pointed to the last entry.

"It says see Bob for the key. So, there must be a Bob."

Everyone looked at each other before Dora spoke.

"Wasn't Grandpa's last horse named Bob?" she asked slowly. "But that can't be the Bob mentioned in the journal.

Jean nodded vigorously.

"Why he sure enough was, but that horse has been dead 4 or 5 years. He lived to be over 20 years old, but he finally died, in fact, on the anniversary of J.D.'s death," she said.

"How did great grandfather die?" asked Betty. "I remember the funeral, but none of the details."

Amos leaned back in his chair and thought for a moment.

"Well, it was August of 1934, he had gone into town for a meeting and when he didn't come home, we went looking for him. He was almost 80 but still rode like a trooper, hating riding in a car. We found him lying alongside the road, Bob was standing by the body, nudging him to get up when we found them," he finally said.

"What happened?" asked Mark, leaning his elbows on the table.

"Well, the sheriff didn't want it to get out, but J.D. had been shot in the back. We told folks that he had had a heart attack and died, but he was murdered," answered Amos.

"Did they catch whoever did it?" asked Karl.

"Sheriff refused to investigate it," responded Amos. "Dane Tucker was a hard, bitter man who did not want the reputation of not being able to solve a crime, so he demanded the real reason he died be hushed up. Since he was the law in these parts, we had no choice."

Amos got to his feet and stretched, hitching up his pants.

"Well, enough about the past," he said, clearing his throat. "Let's go see if we can find where old Bob hid the key to that box."

Led by the old man the entire family made the trek to the stables. Manny Alvarado, the foreman of the ranch, was mending a bridle and looked up in surprise at the delegation entering his territory.

"Senor Puckett, is there something wrong?"

Amos Puckett shock his head.

"No Manny, we came out to look at the tack that my daddy used when he rode old Bob."

Manny stood and pointed down the center area of the stable.

"It is in the tack room where it has been since the Patron died. I still soap and oil it once a week as I did before he died. I will show you."

Walking past the stalls, Manny opened the door to the tack room. Mark was inundated with the smalls of leather and saddle soap as he followed his grandfather into the room where all of the saddles were stored. At the rear of the room was a saddle that was covered with a piece of dark cloth. Jose pulled the cloth away to reveal a very ornate saddle of gleaming dark leather. A matching bridle was hanging form the pommel. Both showed that they had been carefully cared for by Manny, just as he had said.

Almost reverently, Amos ran his hands over the seat of the saddle and then explored the underside with his fingers, looking for any place that a key could be hidden.

"My daddy had this saddle made especially for Bob," said Amos.

As he felt the underside of the saddle, it slipped form its mounting and started to fall to the floor. Mark who was closest, grabbed the saddle horn only to have it come off in his hand.

"Mark, what have you done?" demanded his mother, "you ruined that expensive saddle."

Once again Amos, who had knelt down by the saddle, came to his grandson's defense.

"Leave the boy alone, Dora. He has only found the key, right here where daddy said it would be with old Bob."

The old man got up to show he was holding a safety deposit box key which had been hidden in a recess covered by the saddle horn.

"Good place to hide the key," he commented. When in the tack room it is locked and when he was saddled, no one could ride Bob except my Daddy."

The old man paused, reached up and took down a Stetson hat hanging on a peg above the saddle. He held it out to Mark.

"This was my daddy's hat. See if it fits."

Gingerly, Mark put the black felt hat on his head and found that it fit almost as if it had been made for him.

"Good," nodded Amos Puckett. "Keep it, it's yours."

"Way to go, Mark," said Karl, slapping his older brother on the back. "You found the treasure."

CHAPTER EIGHT
SKELETON CAVE

Once they returned to the house, Amos Puckett and his son left for town to see if there really was a safety deposit box at State National Bank and then to see the bank that wanted to call the note. Now that the excitement was over, Mark felt something of a letdown. At least he had the satisfaction of knowing that he had helped save the ranch.

For a long time, he lay on his bed and day dreamed about the treasure before he decided he need to get up and do something. Bored, he wandered to the kitchen grabbed a couple of carrots and went to see Queenie in the stables. He looked around but found that everyone else seemed to have lain down for naps. It was a hot afternoon. As usual Manny was working on caring for the tack. He glanced up when Mark walked in.

"Everything okay, Mark?" he asked.

"Sure, just came to give Queenie a carrot," the boy responded walking over to where the horse had her head stuck over the lower section of stall door. As she eagerly grabbed the carrot he offered, Mark was struck by a thought.

"Manny," he began, "have you ever heard of Skeleton Cave?"

Manny stopped what he was doing and thought for a few seconds.

"Can't say I have ever heard of skeleton cave, but there is skeleton rock up near the mountains. It still on Puckett land, but it is up in the rear of Spider Canyon."

Mark tried not to show the excitement he felt as he continued to pet Queenie. Maybe he could find Skeleton Cave and the gold.

"How do I get there?" he asked casually.

Manny thought about it for a moment and then pointed toward the mountains.

"Ride due north, about two hours and you should be near the entrance of the canyon. Where did you hear about Skeleton Cave?"

Mark thought fast.

"From one of my grandfather's stories," he responded. "Sounded like a good place to go exploring."

Manny laughed.

"Yeah, I've heard some of his stories. He really gets into them."

Mark finished giving Queenie her carrots and turned.

"Any reason I can't ride up to Skeleton Rock? He asked.

Manny shook his head.

"Well, the only thing is that it will take about an hour to get there and an hour back, so you will only have a little time to look around before it starts to get dark. Might be better to go early in the morning and then you will have all day."

Mark shrugged.

"Well, I know you're probably right, but it is boring and I've nothing to do. At least the ride will occupy my time. You said that I need to ride every day to get good at it."

Manny grinned at the boy.

"I know how that can be. The ranch is great, but at times it can be boring. Okay, just promise me you will be back by sundown."

Mark nodded.

"Oh, I promise, I have no desire to spend a night in the desert."

Manny laughed again and entered the tack room, returning with Queenie's saddle and bridle. Opening the stall door, Mark led Queenie to the crosstie by her halter. She was a docile as a lamb, giving him her usual nuzzle as she hoped for more carrots.

It was only the work of a few minutes to have her saddled and stepping into the saddle as he had been taught, Mark kicked her into a trot as they headed toward the mountains.

It was only a few minutes later that Lucile came strolling into the stables, humming a tune that was popular on the radio.

"Manny, have you seen Mark?" she asked glancing into Queenie's empty stall.

"Sure," replied the foreman. "He rode out of here about ten minutes ago heading for Spider Canyon."

"Manny, you know he will be as lost as a goose when he gets out of sight of the house," she responded.

"Only way he is going to learn is by doing," answered the foreman.

"Will you help me saddle Trinket?" she asked, stepping into the tack room.

She came out lugging her saddle and bridle as Manny led her horse from her stall. Quickly, Lucile saddled and road out after Mark. As she left the yard, Betty and Karl entered the back porch and saw Lucile riding at a gallop toward the north.

Curious that her step-sister would ride off without a word, Betty led the way to the stables where Manny was back at work. He looked up as the two entered the stables.

"Manny, where was Lucile going in such a hurry?" she asked.

Manny straightened and raised one eyebrow.

"Why, she was going after Mark who left about fifteen minutes ago," he said.

"Well, where was he going?" demanded Betty, her hands on her hips.

"He asked about something called Skeleton Cave and I told him about Skeleton Rock up in Spider Canyon. He wanted to ride up there. Is there a problem?"

"Can you help us get a couple of horses saddled?" asked Betty, going into the tack room to retrieve her saddle. She had no intention of letting those two go alone up into the mountains.

When she returned, Manny had led her horse to the crosstie. Karl looked around helplessly, though he had learned to ride in the last few weeks, he had no special horse that he had taken to.

"You want to go to?" asked Manny.

Karl nodded.

Manny stepped to the stall door to another horse and motioned toward the tack room.

"Go get another saddle and bridle, I'll get you a horse."

Quickly both of the teenagers were mounted, and Betty led the way out of the door. As Manny watched, both kicked their horses to a gallop and headed after Mark. Ah, to be young again, he thought as he returned to work.

Mark was enjoying his ride, the wind in his face and the fell of Queenie's muscles working as she bore him along. He felt like he didn't have a care in the world when he heard a yell form behind him. Reigning in Queenie, he turned his horse to see Lucile pounding across the prairie toward him, her long hair billowing out behind her from beneath her own Stetson.

She pulled her horse to a stop beside him.

"Fancy meeting you here," she said favoring him with one of her bewitching smiles.

"Well, what are you doing here?" asked Mark mildly.

"Going with you," she responded. "Spider Canyon is not a place to go alone.

"Well what do you know about Spider Canyon?" he demanded.

"Well, not much, but more than you," she retorted. "My daddy took me there once a long time ago. Why are you going?"

Mark sat his horse deep in thought, finally he responded.

"Well, if you must know, I read in that journal that J.D. Puckett hid the treasure he found, Pancho Villa's gold in Skeleton Cave. Manny told me about Skeleton Rock, and I thought maybe the cave was near the rock."

Lucile nodded thoughtfully.

"Well, that does make a kind of sense. I don't remember a cave, but I do remember daddy pointing out Skeleton Rock. I can at least lead you there."

Mark was secretly pleased to spend some time with the attractive young lady. She wasn't really a cousin, but rather sort of a step cousin, unrelated by blood. He had never really felt comfortable around young ladies of his own age, but he found her very easy to talk to.

"Okay, then lead the way," he finally responded.

Kicking their horses, the two began to ride at a canter across the desert, pulling up when they heard the sounds of hoof beats on the desert ground. Turing, they saw Betty and Karl charging at them. Finally, the four joined up.

"And where do you think you are going?" demanded Betty in some anger. "Without us!"

Mark rubbed his face with one hand while holding the reigns in his right.

"Well, frankly I am looking for Pancho Villa's gold which great granddaddy hid in Skeleton Cave. I read it in that journal that I found."

Betty cocked her head to one side and studied Mark's face for a moment before nodding.

"Fine, let's go," she said kicking her horse into a trot, the other three followed her lead.

Mark had mixed feelings about the group going on the hunt for the gold. The only other group thing he was familiar with was Tommy Irwin and his group, which as his mother pointed out was a gang. This group had a different feeling as there was a blood relationship, except for Lucile and she was kinda like family.

As they rode steadily north, they spotted another group riding toward them. As they got closer, Mark saw that they were three teenagers, but surprisingly they were carrying shovels.

Finally, their paths intersected and both groups reined in their horses just a few feet apart.

"James Harris, what are you doing on Puckett land?" demanded Betty of one of the riders.

The teenager snorted and leered at the young girl. "Well, it soon won't be Puckett land," he responded. "My granddaddy is foreclosing on you trash and if you must know we are looking for treasure."

"Well, do it somewhere else," snapped Betty, her eyes flashing in anger. "This is still Puckett land and has been for three generations."

"Who's going to make us?" demanded one of the other teens backing Harris.

"My daddy!" responded Betty.

"Yeah but he ain't here," returned the pimply faced teen, swinging form the saddle and approaching Betty's horse.

Kicking her heels into her horse, Betty literally rode over the advancing teen. As he fell, his shovel went into the air to be caught by Mark who used it to unseat the second teen who was trying to grab Lucile. The third, James Harris, turned his horse and raced away leaving his two friends lying on the ground, their horses followed the retreating Harris.

Tossing the shovel on the ground, Mark led his group toward Spider Canyon, paying no more attention to the two thugs lying on the ground. As they rode silently, Lucile leaned over and placed her hand on Mark's arm.

"Thank you," she said.

His only response was to smile at her.

It was another thirty minutes before they entered the confines of the canyon. Betty now led the way as they weaved in and out of the huge rocks that littered the floor of the canyon toward its northern wall. Finally, they reined it looking up at a huge boulder balanced on the rim that looked exactly like a Halloween Skeleton's head.

Standing in his stirrups, Mark scanned the area for any signs of a cave but didn't see one. It was Karl who pointed out what seemed to be a rock fall below and to the left of the Skull rock on the canyon rim. Riding closer, Mark saw that what appeared to be a wall of rock actually had an opening at the top.

Dismounting, he handed the reigns to Karl and made his way up the wall of rock to find that the opening was the beginning of a passageway that led into the cliff face. They had found Skeleton Cave.

Climbing back down, Mark returned to Queenie and rummaged in his saddlebags to pull out a small flashlight.

"What are you going to do?" asked Betty, eyeing the light in his hand.

"Go inside the passage and see where it comes out," he responded, starting back up the wall of rocks.

"Not by yourself," responded Lucile, dismounting as she spoke, handing her reigns to Betty and following Mark.

Karl and Betty looked at each other for a moment before both dismounted, tying the four horses to some stunted pines nearby. Soon they scrambled up the rock wall and into the darkness of the passageway.

Mark felt his way along, aided by the flashlight which seemed not as bright inside the passage as it did outside. Finally, he emerged into a large area. Flashing the light around he discovered that this was merely an antechamber to another passage. He turned as he heard someone else emerge from the passage. When she rose to her feet, he saw that it was Lucile, her hair and face smudged with dirt. In a moment another head appeared, and Betty and then finally Karl were standing in the antechamber.

Turning, Mark began to feel his way along the passage until he got to the first side passage. Remembering what it said in the journal, he turned into the side passage and carefully examined the floor until he saw what appeared to be a shovel standing upright in the passageway.

Kneeling down, he ran his hands over the floor and realized that the shovel was merely jammed into the floor. Leaning against the handle, he kept pushing until the shovel came free followed by the sounds of clinking. Holding his flashlight closer, he saw that he had uncovered two old leather saddlebags which were partially split revealing their contents – GOLD.

At that moment, he felt a hand on his shoulder and felt someone's breath on his neck.

"You found it?" breathed Lucile. "My God, you really did find it!"

With her help, Mark was able to get the gold coins safely back to the main passageway where the other two were shocked at the sight of a small mountain of gold twenty-dollar double eagles. The leather saddlebags were partially split from age and exposure to the damp soil, so Mark tore the sleeves off of his shirt to tie them tightly around the bags, keeping the gold from dribbling to the ground. Their problems were solved.

Slowly, he muscled the bags up to the small passageway when he heard a voice echoing from outside.

"Now we've got you brats!" came the taunting voice.

"James Harris!" snorted Betty is distain. "He's a bully and a thief, though no one has ever caught him."

"You can't get away, we've turned your horses loose and we are going to sit here until you have to come out then you are ours!"

In the flashlight, Mark could see Lucile's face, her eyes were big and around. She was clearly terrified.

"What are we going to do?"

CHAPTER NINE
THE RESCUE

Meanwhile, back at the ranch, Amos Puckett and Pete had returned, triumphant. Dora, Margaret and Jean were waiting in the kitchen for their return.

Almost before they could sit down Jean Puckett looked at her husband and demanded to know what happened.

Amos laughed and dumped the bag he was carrying on the table. A veritable river of gold coins spilled across the table, running across the fall on the floor.

"In that safety deposit box was the receipt for repayment of the note and these coins. When I slapped a copy of that receipt on old man Harris' desk, he turned four shades of red, blustered and finally admitted that the bank had misplaced their copy and he thought he could take the ranch since he felt that our copy of the receipt probably was lost when J.D. was killed. He really thought he could get away with it."

"What a crook," exploded Dora.

Amos stopped talking and looked around.

"Where are the kids," he asked. "I wanted to show Mark what his exploring found."

Dora looked at Jean and then at Margaret.

"Why I don't know, we lay down for naps and when we got up, they were not here."

"That's not good," returned Amos getting to his feet. He was out the backdoor before anyone else could get to their feet. He crossed to the stables and quickly found Manny.

"Have you seen the kids?" he demanded.

"They went out riding," responded Manny. "Mark wanted to know about something called Skeleton Cave and I told him that Skeleton Rock was up in Spider Canyon."

At that moment, they both heard a horse come galloping into the yard. Running to the door, they saw that it was Queening, dragging her reins. Something was wrong.

Amos turned to Manny.

"Gather all the men, be ready to ride in twenty minutes."

Quickly he returned to the house and told everyone what had happened. Leaving them abruptly, Amis Puckett went to his gun case, opened the door and took down a pistol belt and strapped it around his hips, filling the holster with a long barreled .45. He looked around when an arm reach past him to grab the second holster resting on the shelf.

"Thought you didn't believe that violence was necessary anymore?" he said to his son.

"Well, sir, that my two girls out there," he responded.

Amos nodded ad led the way back to the kitchen. The sounds of several horses could be heard outside.

Amos looked at the three women.

"We'll be back!"

Reaching the back yard, he found Manny holding the reins of Amos's horse and fifteen other mounted men, all of whom worked on the ranch. A second man led a spare horse and Peter took the reins, swinging into the saddle. With Amos Puckett in the lead, the posse, eighteen strong, headed out for Spider Canyon with blood in their eyes.

As the men rode away, Jean got to her feet, walked to her husband's gun case and grabbed a rifle and a box of ammo. Returning to the kitchen, picked up the phone and rang for the operator.

"Sheriff's office, please."

She waited a moment before continuing.

"This is Jean Puckett, let me talk to that sorry excise for a sheriff."

She waited and finally spoke again.

"Sheriff, this is Jean Puckett. Something has happened to my grandchildren in Spider Canyon. My husband and his men have ridden up their armed to the teeth. I suggest you get your fat ass up there before I get Judge Malone involved."

Hanging up the phone, she got the keys to one of the vehicles from the board just inside the back door. Stopping in the doorway to look at the other two women she grinned.

"Coming, ladies?"

In a few minutes the three were bouncing across the prairie, Spider Canyon bound.

Meanwhile, in Spider Canyon, James Harris and his two side-kicks had built a small fire in the entrance to the rock passage in an attempt to smoke out the four hiding in the cave. They felt that the smoke would make the four have to come out, after all it was getting boring sitting in sun.

For the four sitting in the cave, they thought they were in real trouble when the smoke began to pour into the cave but were delighted when they saw it move to the ceiling and make a trail down the ceiling of the main passage.

Mark studied it for a few minutes before glancing over at his brother Karl.

"What do you think?" he asked, pointing the flashlight toward the smoke.

Karl shrugged.

"Well, it appears to me that there has to be another entrance, which makes this passage act like the flue of a stove," he said.

"Okay, let's find it," said Mark getting to his feet, taking the time to cover the saddlebags with rocks. "This is too heavy to carry, but they may not see it here in the dark."

With the other three following, he led the way down the main passage stopping at the side passage where they had found the gold. Moving down the passage, he grabbed the shovel that his great grandfather had used to mark where he had buried the gold. With it held tightly in his hand, he returned to the three waiting in the main passage and led them on until he found where the smoke was exiting the cave. It was a small hole that looked like it might have been the entrance to some creatures den. Gently, he used the shovel to enlarge the hole until they could squeeze through.

As silently as possible he led the three around the curve of the canyon wall to find that they were behind the three miscreants who were crouched in front of the rock passageway.

"I want that bastard that hit me with that shovel," said one of them, pushing the embers further into the passageway.

"I want that blonde girl that hit me with her horse," said the second one. "I'll make her regret being mean to me."

James Harris just snorted.

"I want to teach them not to mess with the Harris family. Soon as this trash is forced to leave this land, we can find the treasure that I always heard about."

Taking a firm grip on the old shovel he carried, Mark silently approached the three until he was standing just behind them. Raising the shovel, he kicked one down the hill with one booted foot. When the second one jumped to his feet, Mark swung the shovel, hearing a satisfying clang as the shovel connected with the thug's pimply face. He literally flew down the rise. James Harris tried to dive into the passageway to escape, but instead leapt face first into the fire he and his pals had built.

In pain, he forgot about the shovel as he jumped to his feet to frantically brush the embers off of his shirt. With another resounding clang, Mark swung the shovel and hit the bigger boy in the face. Harris went ass over teakettle down the hill to crash into his friends who were just getting to their feet.

With the shovel raised over his head, Mark went charging down the hill. However, Harris pushed himself up on his elbow, clawed a pistol form his waistband and fired at Mark who collapsed, the shovel falling from his hands.

With a scream of rage, Karl grabbed up the shovel Mark had dropped and proceeded to pound Harris until he dropped the pistol, being forced to use his arms to protect his head. Lucile dropped to her knees to check on Mark who was holding his bloody shoulder and moaning.

At that moment the sound of numerous horses echoed through the canyon as the Pucketts and their men came charging from the rocks, rifles being waved in the air. Reaching the group on the ground, Pete jumped from his horse to haul Karl off of James Harris who was bloody from being beaten with the shovel. The other two slowly got to their feet to see that they were surrounded by angry looking armed men, slowly they raised their hands in the air.

"Daddy, they shot Mark!" screamed Lucile when she saw who had arrived. She now had his head in her lap and was trying to stop the bleeding with her little hands.

Climbing up the rise, Amos was the first one to reach his grandson. Pete was close behind and he pulled Lucile and Betty into a hug. Pulling Mark's hand away from his wound, Amos gently opened his shirt to see that the bullet wound was in the left shoulder. The bullet appeared to have entered the front and gone out the back, but it was bleeding heavily. There was no question that they needed to get him to the doctor.

Manny Alvarado walked over to where Karl was threatening to hit Harris with the shovel once again and picked the pistol up off of the ground. He sniffed the barrel and nodded, this was the weapon that had fired the shot that hit Mark.

At that moment two things happened. Sheriff Maddox arrived with four of his deputies, having been at the substation which was only five miles away and Jean Puckett skidded to a stop in the old truck at the bottom of the rise.

"What's going on here?" demanded Mattox as Jean Puckett pushed past him heading for her grandson.

"Shut up you old fool!" snapped Jean as she reached her grandson. Seeing the blood on Mark, she turned toward the men standing by their horses.

"Some of you men come take him down to the truck. We've got to get him to the doctor."

A dozen of the men rushed up the hill and gently lifted Mark, carrying him slowly down to the truck and loading him into the back. Dora Puckett got in the back to be with her son, not surprised to see Lucile climb in with them.

Starting the truck, Jean backed up turned around the roared away.

Once order had been restored, Sheriff Maddox managed to get the whole story out of Betty and Karl and

Manny Alvarado handed him the pistol that James Harris had used to shoot Mark. The sheriff was eyeing the three bloody teens when Amos Puckett confronted him.

"Now Maddox, I want those three arrested for trespass and shooting my grandson, that's attempted murder if you don't know. If you are too afraid of Old Man Harris at the Cattleman's Bank, I can make a phone call and have the Texas Rangers in here to do the job. Am I clear?"

Maddox licked his lips and blustered.

"Who are you to give me orders, Amos Puckett?" demanded the Sheriff. "I'm sheriff in this county."

"And I am the brother-in-law of a state judge and the son of a former Texas Ranger. You also seem to forget that I have a Ranger commission my own self. Unless they are locked up right now, I will arrest them myself and have them taken to Austin for trial."

The two had a staring contest before Maddox dropped his eyes.

"Okay, Puckett," he finally relented. "You win. But old man Harris is going to have a fit at his grandson being arrested."

"Oh, don't worry about him," returned Pete Puckett, his arm around his daughter. "He is going to have his own problems with a little matter of fraud and abuse of legal process."

Maddox opened his mouth and started to say something but thought better of it. With a scowl, Maddox motioned for his deputies to handcuff the three teens and get them out of there. It was going to be tough to ride their horses while handcuffed, but the general consensus was they deserved it.

The Pucketts started to head for their horses when they were stopped by Karl's shrill voice.

"Wait a minute, we can't forget Mark's treasure," he yelled.

Pete and Amos looked at each other and then at Karl.

"Treasure?" asked Amos

"What treasure?" asked Pete.

"Wait here and I will show you," responded Karl darting into the passageway, now clear of embers.

Betty tugged at her father's arm.

"You need to help him daddy, it's heavy and there are two of them," she said as she followed Karl back up the rock wall.

Puzzled, Peete slowly climbed the rock wall himself and squatted down outside the passage way. Pete clearly did not know what to say when Karl's head popped out of the passage. It was very clear that he was struggling to pull something behind him. Joining his nephew, Pete reached into the small passageway and relieved him of the burden he was trying to drag along behind him.

He was surprised to find that whatever Karl had pulled up the incline was heavy. When he finally pulled it free of the passage and saw that it was an old set of large black saddle bags, he really didn't know what to say, but when one of the bags ripped open and a cascade of gold coins spilled out, he was shocked.

"I'll get the second one, Uncle Pete," said Karl disappearing again into the tunnel.

Peter Puckett picked up a handful of the gold coins and looked at his father, who had climbed up beside him, with big eyes.

"So, your story was true?" he said in awe. "This is really Pancho Villa's gold?"

Amos Puckett pushed his Stetson up and summed up things nicely with his response.

"Holy jumping Jehosophat!"

CHAPTER TEN
A DECISION

Mark Phoenix was in pain that much he knew, though he had no idea where he was at the moment. Slowly he opened his eyes to see that his mother's tear streaked face looking down at him. She was clutching his left hand in something close to a death grip.

A glance showed him that his left shoulder was heavily wrapped in bandages. He also saw that Lucile was holding his right hand which he somehow found exciting even in his dreamy state. She smiled that bewitching smile and squeezed his hand tighter. His grandmother was standing at the foot of the bed.

Licking his dry lips, Mark looked up at his mother.

"Where am I?" he asked slowly.

"You are in the hospital, dear," she responded softly. "You were shot."

Mark's mind was sluggish from the drugs he had been given, but finally he remembered what had happened. He had been charging down the hill intending to pound James Harris into the dirt when he heard a loud sound and felt like he had been hit by a train. That was the last thing he really remembered.

He tried to sit up in the bed but winced in pain before giving up. All three women tried to help him at once which meant that none accomplished anything. Finally, his mother found the control for the bed and raised Mark's head.

He had a number of questions he wanted to ask but found himself drifting off and was soon back asleep. The last thing he was aware of was Lucile's hand clutching his.

The next time he opened his eyes, the room of full of people and a face he did not know was looking down at him.

"Well, how are you young fella?" asked the face.

Mark licked his lips and grimaced.

"I guess I'm fine," he responded weakly.

"I'm Doctor Frazier," responded the face. "You were shot but the bullet went in the front and out the back, with no permanent damage."

"How long until I can get out of here?" he asked slowly.

Dr. Frazier studied the chart hanging on the foot of the bed and made a notation.

"Oh, probably a day or so if there is no infection," he responded. "But you will have to take it easy for a week or so as that wound heals. Luckily the bullet did not hit any bones."

Mark nodded and took the straw that Lucile offered him between his dry lips, sucking the water from the glass she held for him. He smiled at her and was rewarded with that bewitching smile of hers. Then a strong hand grabbed his left leg and squeeze.

"How are you doing young fella?" asked his grandfather, his weathered face looking intently at his grandson.

"Fine, sir," responded Mark. "It's a little fuzzy as to what all happened but other than being shot, I guess it was a good day."

Everyone in the room laughed at Mark calling it a good day.

"What all happened?" he asked.

Amos Puckett removed his Stetson and held it in his hand as he took one of the chairs beside the bed.

"Well, after you whipped that Harris boy with the shovel and he shot you, we got there in time to see your brother beating the bejesus out of Harris with the shovel that you had dropped. The Sheriff arrived and arrested those three and your grandmother brought you here."

Mark had a sudden thought and tried to sit up, but instead he groaned and lay back again.

"The treasure, what about the treasure?" he demanded.

"Oh, don't trouble yourself about that boy," responded Amos. "Your brother made sure that we got those two saddlebags, which were my daddy's by the way, and it is safely in the bank."

Amos rubbed his chin thoughtfully before he continued.

"Now a lot has happened since you were brought in here. It has been over two days since they put you in that bed."

"Two days?" demanded Mark in surprise.

Amos nodded.

"Yep," he responded. "Your finding my daddy's journal got a lot of things started. Do you feel up to listening?"

Mark nodded eagerly. He wanted to know what was going on while he was in the bed.

"Well, first off, what we found in that safety deposit box was not only a mess of gold coins, but my Daddy had been building a case against old Man Harris. No one knew about it and if not for the journal, no one would have ever known about it. The records were in the box as well. I made a few calls and the Texas Rangers came in yesterday with a search warrant for Harris' bank and what they found was unbelievable. He's probably going to prison," said Amos.

"Don't forget about the journal, old man," interjected Jean Puckett.

Amos looked at his wife in mock exasperation.

"You want to tell the story, old woman?" he demanded.

"Probably tell it better than you," she retorted.

Amos snorted and shook his head.

"Well, as she said they found a journal kept by the old man. In it was the proof that the Harris family killed my daddy and paid the former sheriff to cover it up. That case is being reopened with Harris and the former sheriff having to answer for the murder and the coverup."

"What were those three thugs doing on the ranch? They kept talking about looking for treasure, but how did they know?" asked Mark.

Peter Puckett spoke up at this point.

"Let me answer that, daddy," he said, stepping up beside the bed.

"First off, Mark," he began. "I want to thank you for saving my two girls. Those three admitted that they planned to kill all of you and take the treasure they thought you had found to Mexico."

"But how did they know about the treasure?" asked Mark again.

"Oh, granddaddy's old partner was Ned Harris, Old man Harris' cousin. According to the journal after the two of them found the treasure, while Daddy was in town, Ned contacted his cousin and they cooked up the plan for Ned to murder Granddaddy and they would launder the gold through the bank. So, they knew about the gold but not where granddaddy hid it after he was forced to kill Ned. They did suspect it was somewhere north of the ranch."

He paused as Lucile forced the straw between Mark's lips again. He gratefully took a long sip before laying back again.

"Now the bank examiners are due in here tomorrow to examine the books and some of the things that old man Harris has been up to. The Rangers have taken charge of your three friends and the Sheriff may well have some questions to answer as well. So, you all stirred up quite a hornet's nest."

At that moment, the door to the room opened once again and two men came in. One was dressed in a suit and carried a dark leather briefcase while the other was dressed like a cowboy with a big Texas Ranger Badge pinned on his chest. His grandfather rose to meet them and the three shook hands.

The Ranger approached the bed and looked down at the boy.

"Boy, my name is Bart Delacroix and I am a Captain in the Texas Rangers. I wanted to come and shake your hand," the Ranger said offering his hand. Mark offered his own hand which was engulfed in the Ranger's huge hand.

"Are you feeling up to some conversation?" he asked.

Mark nodded curiously. Why would a Texas Ranger want to talk to him?

"Good," he responded. "Well, Amos here told me about you finding J.D. Puckett's journal. I want to tell you that you have no idea what you set in motion. This here is Colonel Archie Bancroft from Military Intelligence. Some of what we found in the bank required that we bring in the military.

You see, the Cattlemen's Bank has been acting as a listening post, you might call it, for those in Mexico who would like to see us lose the war. So, your actions have led to a number of results."

Colonel Bancroft nodded as the Ranger spoke.

"That's true, young man. Because of your actions, we are in the process of breaking what we think is a major spy ring along the border. In the last two days there have been a number of arrests."

Mark finally got up the courage to ask the question that was foremost in his mind.

"Since you are from the military, I guess you are here to take the treasure, Pancho Villa's gold. It was originally stolen form the military, so I guess it goes back to the military."

Bancroft smiled and shook his head.

"No, I am afraid you are stuck with that mountain of gold. Even though legend says that it was stolen from an army paymaster by Pancho Villa, there are no records confirming that, so the U.S. Army has no claim on it. It's up to the state of Texas to decide if they have a claim on the gold," he responded.

At that Mark looked at the Ranger.

Ranger Delacroix smiled and shook his head.

"Nope, the state of Texas has no claim on the gold either. As far as anyone is concerned, it was the property of J.D. Puckett and it goes to his heirs. Just don't spend it all in one place."

Opening his briefcase, Bancroft pulled a binder and a small box from the interior and held it out to Mark.

"Mark, one other thing," he began. "On behalf of the President of the United States I want to present you with this certificate and a medal for being instrumental in breaking the spy ring."

Not to be outdone, Ranger Delacroix pulled a small box out of his pocket.

"From the state of Texas, you are now made an honorary Texas Ranger. Those of us old enough to remember him thought to world of J.D. Puckett and finally his killers can be brought to justice thanks to you."

Leaning forward, Delacroix pinned the badge on Mark's hospital gown and shook his hand.

Delacroix smiled at the four teenagers.

"You know back in the 1880s when the Rangers were the law in Texas, we were known for riding forever to bring back a bad guy. We were called the long riders, I guess we can call you four the young riders"

With that the Ranger and the Colonel took their leave. The family gathered round the bed again.

Amos Puckett once again became the spokesman.

"Now, Mark," he began, his face solemn. "About the treasure or Pancho Villa's gold as you call it."

Mark's face fell. From his grandfather's tone of voice, he was sure that they would not get to keep the treasure.

"Well, the coins have a larger value to collectors than the face value, so when all are sold, I reckon it will come to something over $250,000.00. That's a lot of money by anybody's reckoning.

There were two other possible claimants to the gold, the State of Texas and the U.S. Army. As you heard both have denied any claim on the gold, so it is left to the family."

Mark looked at his grandfather expectantly.

"Yes sir?"

"Oh, don't keep the boy in suspense, old man" urged his grandmother.

Amos Puckett finally grinned at his grandson.

"Well, we had a family discussion last night and made a decision. You saved the ranch by finding that journal and tracking down where daddy hid the receipt for paying off the loan. You also saved Betty and Lucile from those ruffians, you and your brother.

So, by mutual agreement half of the treasure is being put into a trust for you. It will start paying out to you when you reach twenty-one years of age or when you marry whichever comes first."

Mark was overwhelmed, he had never dreamed of having so much money, but he had to be fair.

"But grandfather, we were all involved in finding the treasure, so it hardly seems fair that I get half."

"Mark, it was all you," objected Lucile. "Without you finding that hidden room in the old dugout and your finding the journal and then deciding to go riding off by yourself, none of this would have happened."

"That's right, Mark," added Betty. 'You are the reason the treasure was found. Otherwise it would still be buried in the cave."

"Sorry, boy," added Amos. "It does you credit to want to be fair, but everyone is in agreement, half of it is yours. As for the other half, it will be equally divided between Karl, Betty and Lucile."

As Mark was mentally adjusting to being what he considered rich, his mother spoke up.

"Mark, my father's attorney finished writing the trust yesterday and the trust document also says that if needed part of the funds can be used to pay for your care, so if you still want to do so we can move back to New York City. We can get a very nice apartment near Central Park. It's your choice."

Mark was stunned, he had believed that he would never get back to New York, now he could go back in style. Slowly he looked around at all of the faces surrounding his hospital bed and then thought about all of the friends he had left in New York. Finally, he made his decision.

"Well, mom, I do miss the city, but the friends I have made here are better friends that I left behind."

He looked at Lucile and surprisingly blushed red.

"A month ago, I would have said New York City in a minute. But now, after all that has happened, I guess I want to stay here. After all, as the Ranger said, we are the young riders and I do like to ride a horse. Why in New York City I could only ride in the park. Here I can ride anywhere."

Looking around at all of the happy faces, Mark realized that he had found a home. If his father was here, it would be perfect.